Note to parents, carers and teachers

Read it yourself is a series of modern stories, favourite characters and traditional tales written in a simple way for children who are learning to read. The books can be read independently or as part of a guided reading session.

Each book is carefully structured to include many high-frequency words vital for first reading. The sentences on each page are supported closely by pictures to help with understanding, and to offer lively details to talk about.

The books are graded into four levels that progressively introduce wider vocabulary and longer stories as a reader's ability and confidence grows.

Ideas for use

- Begin by looking through the book and talking about the pictures. Has your child heard this story before?

- Help your child with any words he does not know, either by helping him to sound them out or supplying them yourself.

- Developing readers can be concentrating so hard on the words that they sometimes don't fully grasp the meaning of what they're reading. Answering the puzzle questions at the end of the book will help with understanding.

For more information and advice on Read it yourself and book banding, visit www.ladybird.com/readityourself

Book Band 5

Level 1 is ideal for children who have received some initial reading instruction. Each story is told very simply, using a small number of frequently repeated words.

Special features:

Peppa

Mummy Pig

George

Daddy Pig

swimming pool

Opening pages introduce key story words

Rebecca Rabbit

Richard Rabbit

watering can

6

7

"Here, let me help you," says Daddy.

Splash! George gets in the pool. He is not scared.

Large, clear type

12

13

Careful match between story and pictures

Educational Consultant: Geraldine Taylor
Book Banding Consultant: Kate Ruttle

LADYBIRD BOOKS

UK | USA | Canada | Ireland | Australia
India | New Zealand | South Africa

Ladybird Books is part of the Penguin Random House group of companies
whose addresses can be found at global.penguinrandomhouse.com.

ladybird.com

Text adapted from Peppa Goes Swimming, first published by Ladybird Books, 2009
This edition first published by Ladybird Books, 2016
001

Text and illustrations copyright © Astley Baker Davies Ltd/Entertainment One UK Ltd, 2016
Adapted by Ellen Philpott
The moral right of the author has been asserted

This book is based on the
TV Series 'Peppa Pig'
'Peppa Pig' is created by
Neville Astley and Mark Baker
Peppa Pig © Astley Baker Davies Ltd/
Entertainment One UK Ltd, 2003

www.peppapig.com

Printed in China

A CIP catalogue record for this book is
available from the British Library

ISBN: 978-0-241-24432-6

Going
Swimming

Adaptation written by Ellen Philpott
Based on the TV series *Peppa Pig*. *Peppa Pig* is
created by Neville Astley and Mark Baker

Peppa

 George

Daddy Pig

 watering can

Mummy Pig

 **swimming pool**

Rebecca Rabbit

Richard Rabbit

Peppa and George are at the swimming pool with Mummy and Daddy Pig.

Peppa loves swimming.

9

Peppa gets in the
swimming pool.

George is scared.
He will not get in.

"Here, let me help you," says Daddy.

Splash! George gets in the pool. He is not scared.

Richard and Rebecca Rabbit
are at the swimming pool
with Mummy Rabbit.

"We love swimming,"
says Rebecca.

"Try kicking in the water, George. It will help you," says Mummy Pig.

George and Richard try kicking in the water.

"Oops! Try not to splash us!"
says Daddy Pig.

Everybody gets splashed.
George and Richard love
splashing.

"Look! George and Richard are good at kicking," says Peppa to Rebecca.

"We are good at swimming!" says Rebecca.

Peppa and Rebecca go
up and down the pool.

"Look at us, George!"
says Peppa.

Richard has a watering can.
Oops! He has let it go.

Daddy Pig swims down to
get the watering can.

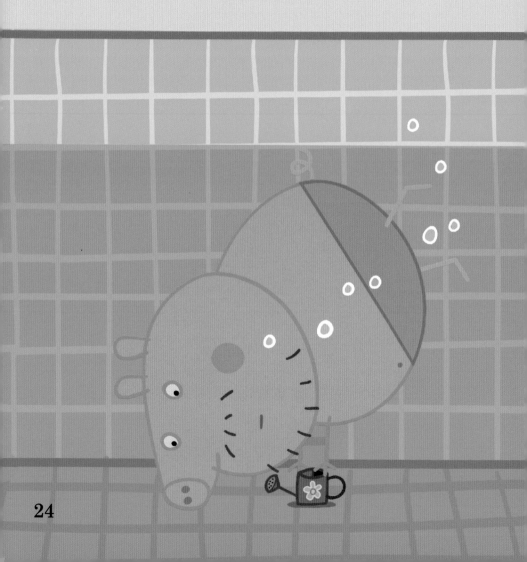

Daddy Pig is good
at swimming.

"Here you go, Richard,"
says Daddy Pig.

Oops! Richard is splashing
Daddy Pig with the
watering can!

"Try not to splash me!"
says Daddy.

Everybody loves swimming!

How much do you remember about the story of Peppa Pig: Going Swimming? Answer these questions and find out!

- Who does not want to get in the swimming pool?

- Who does Peppa see at the swimming pool?

- What toy does Richard drop in the pool?

- Who gets the toy back out?

Look at the pictures from the story and say the order they should go in.

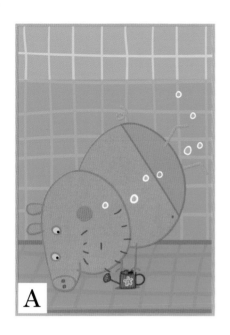

A

B

C

D

Tick the books you've read!

Level 1

Level 2

The Read it yourself with Ladybird app is now available